Hinsdale Public Library · Founded 1892

A Gift To The Library From

The Hinsdale Junior
Woman's Club
In Honor of the Birth of
Jackson Paul Ovnik

Hinsdale Public Library
Hinsdale, Illinois 60521

My name is Seymour Sleuth. I am the greatest
detective in the world. With my faithful assistant
and photographer, Abbott Muggs, I travel around the world
solving mysteries. This is a casebook of one of my
most baffling mysteries. I call it <u>The</u> <u>Mystery</u> <u>of</u>
<u>King</u> <u>Karfu</u>.

Welcome!

to the
Tomb of
King Karfu

Mediterranean Sea

★ Cairo

the tomb of
King Karfu

Nile River

Egypt

The Mystery of King Karfu

story and pictures
by Doug Cushman

![HarperCollins] **HarperCollins**Publishers

The Stone Chicken
of King Karfu

June 24, 8:14 A.M., London, England— While finishing a little breakfast with Muggs, I receive a telegram from my good friend Professor Slagbottom.

Big Ben O'Gram
"ALWAYS ON TIME"

Seymour,

Please come to Egypt at once! My latest discovery-the Stone Chicken of King Karfu-has been stolen! I am sending two tickets for the ship the Sea Pharaoh. Meet me at the King's Tomb and help solve this mystery!

-Professor Slagbottom

Same day, 10:36 A.M. — Muggs agrees to come with me to photograph every moment of this case. After a light snack, we pack our bags and take a taxi to the dock where the <u>Sea Pharaoh</u> is waiting.

Piccadilly Taxi
Receipt

£4.00

June 24
1928

Packing List

✓tie   ✓fish
✓sandwiches   ✓chips
✓suntan lotion ✓underwear
✓pants   ✓toothbrush
✓candy bar   ✓hat

·Visa·

Seymour Sleuth
name

World's Greatest Detective
occupation

wombat   Australia
species   birthplace

May 4, 1888
birthday

June 24, 1928
issue date

·Visa·

Abbott Muggs
name

Photographer
occupation

mouse   England
species   birthplace

September 24, 1898
birthday

June 24, 1928
issue date

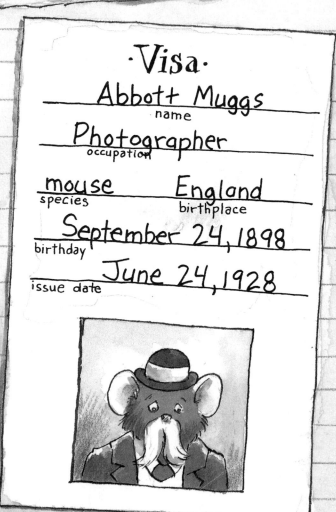

June 25-27, Aboard the <u>Sea Pharaoh</u> — I relax and read about Professor Slagbottom's discovery. The Stone Chicken is believed to be an important clue to the famous Lost Treasure of King Karfu. King Karfu was a gourmet cook as well as a wealthy pharaoh with many treasures. His greatest treasure was hidden in a golden box that has been missing for centuries. No one knows what the treasure is, but whoever has the Chicken may be able to find it!

June 27, 9:48 A.M., Cairo— The <u>Sea Pharaoh</u> docks
in Cairo. Muggs and I ride camels to the Tomb
of King Karfu. The tomb is magnificent. My
camel ride is not.

U · Rent · a · Camel
14 King Tut Way · Cairo, Egypt

2 camels @ £ 19.35

PAID

"Ride in style along the Nile"

The professor's camp at the tomb

Same day, 11:38 A.M., The Tomb of King Karfu— I meet my friend Professor Slagbottom. "I was in my tent late at night studying the Chicken," he explains. "I went to the food tent for a cup of tea. I was only gone a few minutes. When I returned to my tent, the Chicken was gone!"

"What about the Lost Treasure of King Karfu?" I ask. "Isn't it true that whoever stole the Chicken will be able to find the Lost Treasure?"

"That's right," says the professor. "There is a secret code written on the Chicken. I was just starting to decode it when the Chicken was stolen. We must hurry, or the thief will be able to steal the Lost Treasure too!"

Same day, 11:54 A.M. — I go to the professor's tent and view the scene of the crime. Muggs takes pictures of the clues we find.

footprint

red fish

scrap of paper

crumbs

Notes on the Suspects

Professor Slagbottom gives me a list of the others who were working near the tomb at the time of the crime. They were the only ones around the tomb that night. One of them must be the thief.

THE COOK
- has cooked for Professor Slagbottom for many years
- is usually cranky
- likes to keep to himself

DR. AMOS RAMSDELL
- expert on Egypt
- old rival of Professor Slagbottom
- visiting tomb to collect treasures for his museum

JANET SLUGG
- art student
- studied Egyptian art in school
- recently joined Professor Slagbottom's crew

Same day, lunchtime — I sit down to a small lunch and interview the cook.

"Where were you when the Chicken was stolen?" I ask him.

"I was looking through my recipes while my cookies were baking," he says. "I'm a cook, not a thief! Besides, I can't read that funny writing on the Chicken. Why would I want that old Chicken? All I want is to build my own restaurant someday."

The cook's footprint

(Note: His couscous is excellent.)

butter
salt

⅔ C couscous
1 C water
Boil water with salt. Add couscous and butter. Cover and take off heat. Let sit for 5 minutes. Serve hot.

Same day, 3:17 P.M. — I watch Janet Slugg at work. "I was sketching a mummy when the Chicken was stolen," she says. "What would I want with the Chicken anyway? Just because I studied the secret code in school doesn't make me a thief. I'm a poor artist, not a crook! I need this job to pay for my art classes." She always drinks tea and eats cookies while she works (she does not offer me any!). Could such a young artist be a thief?

Janet Slugg's footprint

Same day, 4:10 P.M. — I watch Dr. Ramsdell. He knows the tomb — and the secret code — very well. He says, "I would love to have the Stone Chicken for my museum, but I would never steal it. I'm a scholar, not a thief!"

He drinks tea and eats peanut butter and celery when he works (he doesn't offer me any of those either!).

Dr. Ramsdell's footprint

Same day, 6:33 P.M. — Muggs and I go back to my tent and have a small bite to eat. I look over my notes about this baffling case. Is someone lying? Have I missed a clue?

I decide to give this case careful thought.

cookies + footprints + fish = ?

I'm hungry!

Slugg ⟶ cook?
⤷   ↑
Ramsdell ?

Notes on the Clues

FOOTPRINT
- matches the cook's foot
- does not match Dr. Ramsdell's foot
- matches Janet Slugg's foot

CRUMBS
- found with the cook
- Dr. Ramsdell usually eats peanut butter and celery, doesn't leave crumbs
- found with Janet Slugg

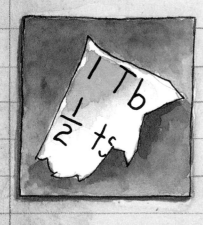

SCRAP OF PAPER
- I've seen something like it before, but I can't remember where
- Is it important?

RED FISH
- I dismiss this clue. It was a herring from the sandwich I brought for my lunch.

Notes on the Suspects

THE COOK
- foot matches print at scene of crime
- bakes cookies
- can't read secret code

DR. RAMSDELL
- foot does not match print at scene of crime
- drinks tea and eats peanut butter and celery
- can read secret code

JANET SLUGG
- foot matches print at scene of crime
- eats cookies
- can read secret code

That night, 9:47 p.m. — A message from the professor arrives at my tent.

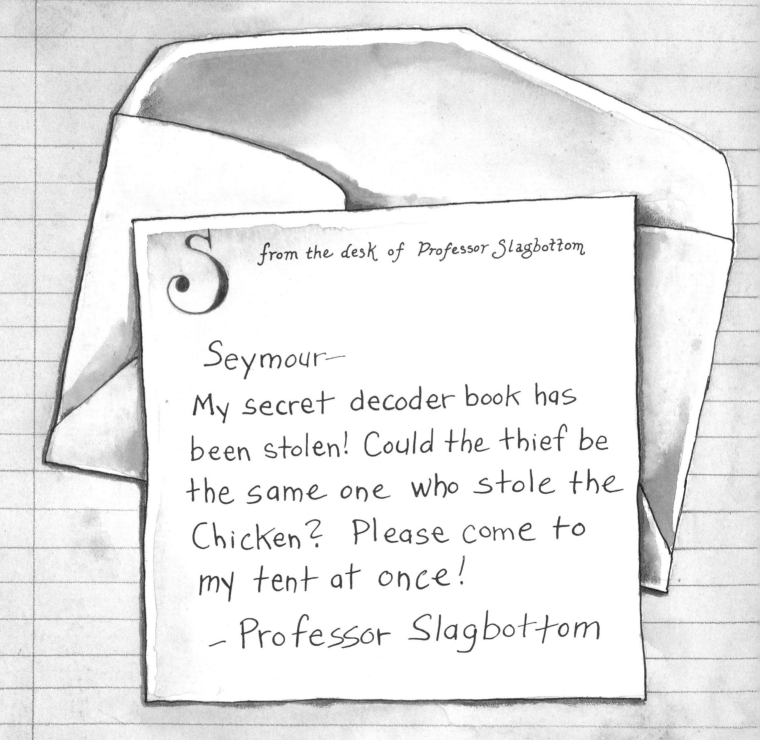

from the desk of Professor Slagbottom

Seymour—

My secret decoder book has been stolen! Could the thief be the same one who stole the Chicken? Please come to my tent at once!

— Professor Slagbottom

There is only one person who would need the decoder book. I know who the thief is!

Later that night, 9:55 P.M. — Muggs and I tell the professor, then we all sneak up to the thief's tent.

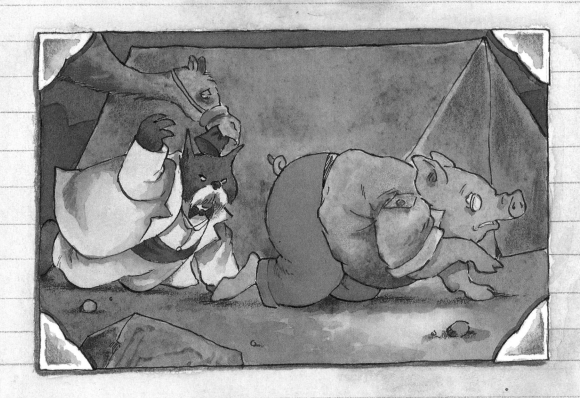

We hear a noise, but it is only my stomach growling.

We burst into the thief's tent and find...

The cook! Caught red-handed with the Stone Chicken and the decoder book!

But before we can stop him, he jumps on his camel and tries to escape.

My expert camel riding brings the crook to justice.

Same night, 11:13 P.M., Police Station — The police arrive and take the cook to jail. He confesses to the crime. The professor is happy to have the Chicken back.

Fingerprint File

Name _____ the cook

thumb   right index   middle   pinky

Police Department
Confession Form EZ-96

I, the cook, stole the Stone Chicken of King Karfu and the professor's decoder book. I wanted to find the Lost Treasure of King Karfu so I could sell it and use the money to build my own restaurant. I am sick of cooking for Professor Slagbottom!

Signed _____The Cook_____

But the case is not over yet.

June 28, 10:36 A.M., Back at the Tomb—
The professor has finished
translating the secret code on
the Chicken.

At last we know how to find
the Lost Treasure of
King Karfu!

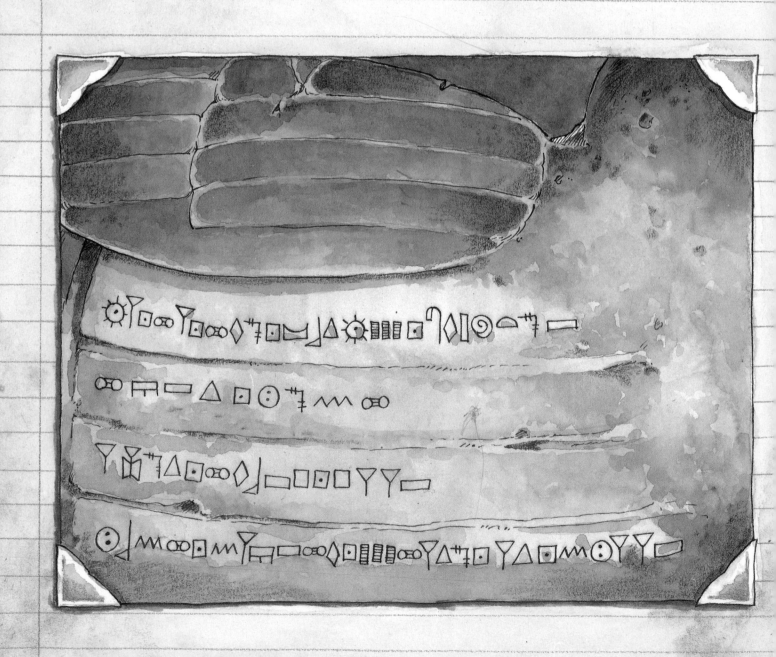

KEY TO THE SECRET CODE

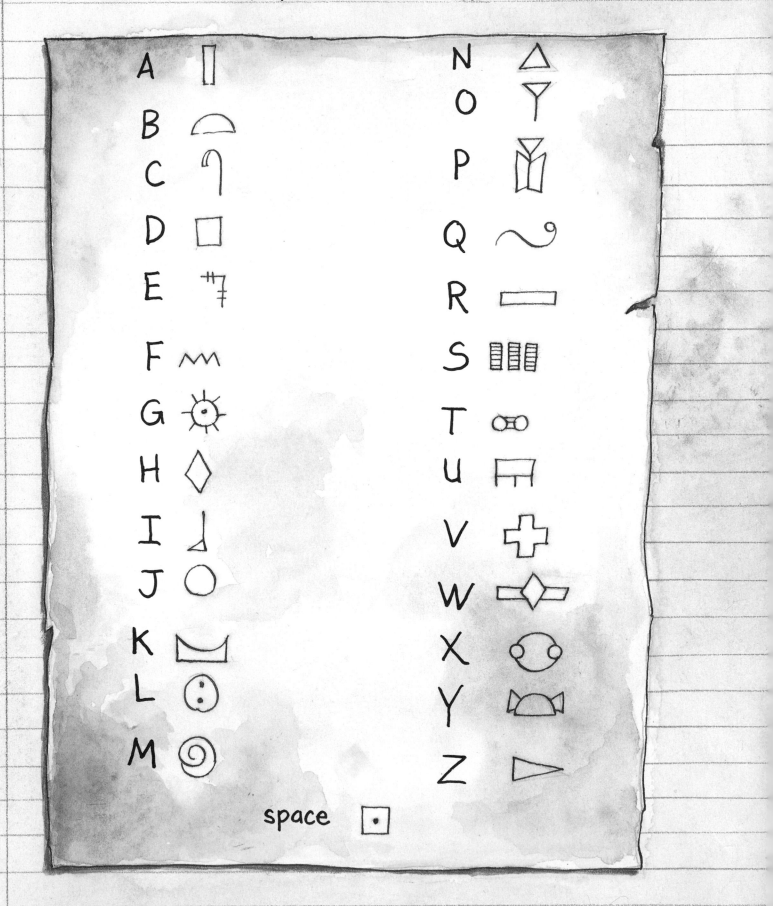

Same morning, 10:51 A.M. — Following the directions, we start at the entrance of the tomb. I graciously suggest that the professor go into the deep, dark, and spooky tunnel first while I stand guard outside. He says I should go first.

We flip a coin.

I lose.

I let Muggs go in first.

We enter the King's Chamber.

We turn left.

We open the third door.

We lift the fourth stone in the floor.

The Chicken was right! We find a golden box.
It must be the Lost Treasure!

Same day, 1:30 P.M. — The professor opens the golden box. Inside are sheets of parchment. He examines one carefully.

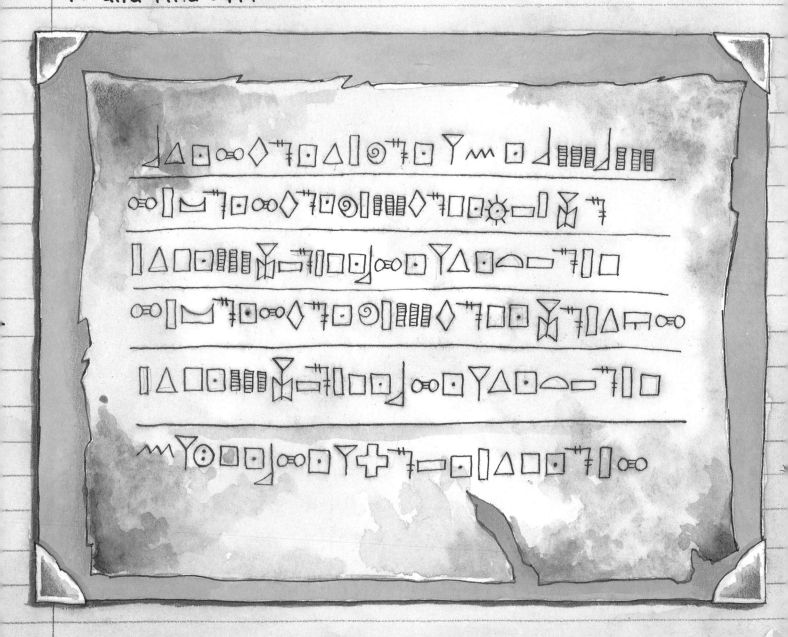

"What is it?" I ask.

"I believe it is a recipe", he says. "If it is, we have found what King Karfu would have treasured the most — his own secret recipes! Let's decode it and find out."

Same day, 3:26 P.M. — "Eureka!" the professor cries. "There is no question that this is the Lost Treasure of King Karfu — this recipe is delicious!"

I agree with the professor. I've solved many mysteries, but this is the tastiest one yet!

The Nile Gazette

"All the news that prints" • June 28, 1928 • Late Edition

SEYMOUR SLEUTH DOES IT AGAIN

Great Detective Solves Mystery of Stone Chicken and Helps Discover the Lost Treasure of King Karfu

(Egypt) Master detective Seymour Sleuth has solved the baffling mystery of the missing Stone Chicken of King Karfu. The thief was apprehended late last night after a high-speed camel chase. No one was injured, although one of the camels sustained a slight bruise to the knee. "All in all it was a very delicious conclusion to a troublesome case," the detective said. "There were times when I thought I couldn't do it. But we had some lucky breaks..."

The detective thanked his assistant, Abbott Muggs, for his help. "It's always a pleasure to help a great detective," said Muggs. "Besides, Seymour always knows the best places to eat."

The vile criminal was the cook of the expedition. He confessed that the

(see page 7, column 2)

For Sally Doherty
who believed in the
Lost Treasure from
the beginning

The Mystery of King Karfu
Copyright © 1996 by Doug Cushman
Printed in the U.S.A. All rights reserved.

Library of Congress Cataloging-in-Publication Data
Cushman, Doug.
The mystery of King Karfu / story and pictures by Doug Cushman.
p.   cm.
Summary: The great detective Seymour Sleuth and his assistant Muggs journey to Egypt to search for a missing stone chicken, an important clue to the Lost Treasure of King Karfu.
ISBN 0-06-024796-7. — ISBN 0-06-024797-5 (lib. bdg.)
(1. Egypt—Fiction. 2. Mystery and detective stories.)
I. Title.   II. Series.
PZ7.C959My 1996
[E]—dc20
95-31064
CIP
AC

1 2 3 4 5 6 7 8 9 10
First Edition